SOLO
The Homeless

Home Farm Twins

Solo

The Homeless

Jenny Oldfield

Illustrated by Kate Aldous

Hodder
Children's
Books

a division of Hodder Headline plc

A Catalogue record for this book is available from the British Library

ISBN 0 340 74388 3

Typeset by Avon Dataset Ltd, Bidford-on-Avon, Warks

Printed and bound in Great Britain by
The Guernsey Press Co. Ltd, Guernsey, Channel Islands

Hodder Children's Books
a division of Hodder Headline plc
338 Euston Road
London NW1 3BH

One

'What a lovely life!' Hannah Moore lay flat on her back looking up at a blue sky. Long grass brushed her bare arms; Speckle the dog snuffled her face.

'What a brilliant summer!' her twin sister, Helen, agreed. 'Home Farm is full of animals!'

'Hey, Speckle, that tickles!' Hannah pushed him off and rolled on to her stomach next to Helen. Then they began to list the animals living with them in their new home.

'Lucy and Dandy, six hens, four kittens.'

'Sugar and Spice, Sal, Speckle.'

Speckle wagged his tail.

1

'Lucy laid two eggs this morning.'

'One of the kittens escaped from the barn.'

'Sal kept Dad awake all night.'

Helen grinned. 'The whole place has come alive!'

'Full to overflowing.'

'Oh, I wouldn't say that.' Helen rested her chin on her hands and peered through spears of long grass at the Saunders' pony grazing in his paddock.

'No, I suppose we do have room for a few more.'

'If Mum and Dad will let us.'

'If we come across another rabbit we could rescue, for instance.'

'Or a ferret we could foster.'

'After all, we've got a goat to guard us.'

'And kittens to care for.'

Hannah left a pause. 'What do you do with hens?' she wondered.

'I don't know. Anyway, we've got a farm full of animals,' Helen sighed. 'That's what counts.'

Home Farm had become a real farm again since the Moore family had moved into the old place on the fellside overlooking Doveton Lake. Sal the goat gave them milk, the hens laid eggs. The twins' mother, Mary, used the eggs in her little café in Nesfield. Now

Lucy the goose had started laying too.

'Maybe we could have a sheep,' Hannah suggested. 'Or two, or three.'

'Or a cow.'

'Or a pony.' She gazed at the lovely pale grey pony between the bars of the paddock fence.

'Dream on.' Helen cut her short.

'Why not? Why couldn't we have a pony?'

'Trust you to think big.'

'What do you mean?' Hannah frowned and sat up. 'Sal's nearly as big as a pony, in case you hadn't noticed. And a whole lot noisier.' Sal often brayed in her field all night long.

'Yes, but a goat's useful, isn't it? Mum can use the milk.' Helen didn't dare to dream about having a pony – a beautiful one with soft eyes, a flowing mane, who ran swift as the wind . . . 'All our animals are useful, that's why she said we could have them.' Their mum was down-to-earth about such things.

'Sugar and Spice aren't,' Hannah pointed out. 'You can't do anything with rabbits.'

'Mum will soon think of something.' Mary Moore always found a use for things; old planks of wood, bits of old bicycles, jumble-sale curtains.

Hannah gave up the argument. She concentrated instead on the pony. 'Lucky thing!' she sighed, as she pulled up a handful of juicy grass and went up to the fence. Speckle trotted after her.

'Who?'

'Whoever owns this pony.' The paddock belonged to the Saunders family at Doveton Manor. It stood right on the edge of the village. Now the grey pony pricked up his ears and strolled towards her.

'He is . . .' Helen searched for the best word. He was light grey, almost silvery white, with a long, pure white mane.

'Gorgeous, brilliant, amazing, wonderful!'

'Right.'

They gazed into his big brown eyes. Hannah felt his soft muzzle brush the palm of her hand as he whisked the grass into his mouth. He munched happily. It was high summer, the fields were full of buttercups, the house shimmered in the heat.

'Solo!' A shimmery figure suddenly strode into the field. The pony whinnied and turned his head.

'That's his name, Solo,' Hannah whispered.

'It suits him.' Helen stretched out her arm to give him a gentle pat on the neck.

The figure came closer. It was a girl they'd never seen before. She looked older than the twins, taller, with corn-yellow hair pushed back from her face by a black band. She wore a white T-shirt and light-coloured jodhpurs with black boots. 'Solo, didn't you hear me call?' She told the pony off with a light, musical voice. He tossed his mane and went to meet her. Helen and Hannah backed away from the fence, while Speckle waited quietly beside them.

'Hi, I'm Laura Saunders.' The girl's smile was warm and friendly. 'You must be the twins from Home Farm.'

Helen nodded and pushed her thick black hair behind her ears. 'I'm Helen.'

'And I'm Hannah.' They stood in the hot sun feeling awkward. Laura looked cool and relaxed. Hannah stared down at her crumpled T-shirt and cut-off jeans with frayed hems.

'Mummy and Daddy told me all about you. This must be Speckle?' Laura put an arm round Solo's neck and led him up to the fence again. Speckle's tail wagged as he heard his name. 'I was away on a school trip when they first met you and Sinbad.'

'The runaway cat.' Helen remembered all too well

the time when Sinbad had paid a visit to Doveton Manor.

As they talked, Solo reached over the fence and nuzzled Hannah's pocket.

'Sorry, there's nothing in there for you!' she laughed. She turned it inside out. 'He's lovely,' she told Laura. 'We were just saying, we'd love to have a pony at Home Farm.'

'He is lovely, isn't he?' Laura agreed. 'I always used to think he was the best pony in the world.'

'Used to?' Helen was puzzled. 'Isn't he still?'

'Well, when I say the best pony, I suppose Solo is still that.' Laura paused and bit her lip with excitement. 'Do you like horses?' she asked the twins.

'We love them!' they said together.

'Would you like me to show you something?' Her eyes lit up with a secret she couldn't keep.

They nodded.

'Climb over the fence then.'

'Can Speckle come too?' Helen checked.

'Of course he can.' Laura led the way, her long legs striding over the paddock, the twins and Speckle trotting to keep up. 'Now Solo, you have to stay here.' She vaulted the gate and waited. 'Be a good boy.'

As she climbed the gate, Hannah glanced behind. Solo stood alone in the paddock, pawing the ground with his front hoof.

'Come on!' Laura could hardly wait. She took them across an empty yard towards a small stable block. 'Come and see what I got for my birthday. It's the best present I've ever had in my whole life. Just you wait!'

She opened the stable door and they stepped into an airy room. It was divided into two, with saddles and bridles hanging from one wall, and a wooden stall in the far corner. Inside the stall there was a manger full of hay and straw on the floor.

'Sultan!' Laura called softly. 'He's only just arrived,' she explained to the twins. 'He's still a bit nervous.'

Hidden by the wooden wall, Sultan shifted and blew through his nose. Laura beckoned them forward.

Hannah and Helen went quietly. Inside the stall was a horse so big, so brown, so beautiful that he took their breath away.

When he saw them, Sultan tossed his head and tried to shy away.

'Steady, boy.' Laura waited for him to settle. 'He got here yesterday morning, a complete surprise. Daddy says it'll take a day or two for him to get used to us. He's five years old, over fifteen hands. I can still hardly believe it!'

'Lucky thing!' Helen whispered enviously. She couldn't help herself.

Hannah dug her in the ribs. 'He's lovely,' she said politely. Sultan had laid back his ears as if he didn't like being stared at by strangers.

'I was just about to take him into the paddock to meet Solo.' Carefully Laura unbolted the stall door and caught hold of Sultan's halter. He tossed his head, then let himself be led out into the tack room past the twins. They didn't even reach to his shiny brown shoulder. Out in the yard, when the sun caught his velvety coat, it shone and gleamed bright chestnut.

'Wow!' Helen glanced at Hannah.

'Some horse!'

'Big.'

'Massive.'

Laura was having trouble leading him by a halter into the paddock. The twins and Speckle stood well to one side. 'Could you open the gate, please?' she called.

Hannah lifted the latch. Helen held on to Speckle so that he didn't get in the way.

At last Laura guided the big thoroughbred through the gate. 'He's a bit of a handful at the moment, but that's because he's young. Daddy says that Sultan has a good eye and he's well-schooled, only he's bound to be a bit edgy at first.'

Sultan picked his forelegs high off the ground, then skittered sideways across the field. 'Steady, boy.' Laura handled him well and spoke patiently as Hannah closed the gate. Then they all stood back.

'You see what I mean?' Laura turned to them with a proud smile. 'Solo may be the best pony you could wish for, but Sultan is going to be even better.' Gradually she let out the halter rope, watching him carefully.

'How is he better?' Hannah could see that of course he was bigger than the silver-grey pony. Solo had kept his distance, trotting up and down the far side of the field.

'Well, for a start he's a thoroughbred.' Laura saw that she would have to explain slowly. 'That means he's specially bred to keep his blood pure, with all the best points. See his head – it's nice and flat and bony.

That's good in a horse. And he's got nice small ears, and a long neck.'

'Long legs.' Helen compared Sultan's slim ones with Solo's stumpier figure.

'Shh, he'll hear you.' Hannah thought poor Solo looked put-out. Laura made such a fuss of the elegant Sultan that she completely ignored her old friend.

Helen tutted. 'He can't understand what we're talking about.'

'Want to bet?'

Laura laughed. 'Poor old Solo, he's bound to be a bit jealous, I suppose.'

Hannah nodded hard.

'Would you hold Sultan for me while I go and fetch him?'

Helen stepped forward.

'It's OK, he won't bite.' Laura handed her the halter rope, then went to get Solo. He came trotting obediently to her call, pleased to have her attention at last. He came up and nuzzled her shoulder, then jerked his head towards the magnificent newcomer, as if to say, 'Who's this?'

'That's Sultan,' she announced. She brought them closer. The thoroughbred side-stepped nervously and tossed his mane. Helen held on tight.

Solo looked his new companion up and down. He gave a flick of his long white tail.

'That's a good boy, Solo. You two can be friends. It'll be good for you.'

They held their breath and watched as Solo stayed close at Laura's side and Sultan surveyed his new field.

'Let's let Sultan off,' Laura decided at last, slipping the halter over Sultan's head. 'Come on, this is where you live from now on!'

'Stay!' Hannah said to Speckle. The dog sat glued to the spot. 'Good boy.'

Sultan flicked his heels, his ears went up, he trotted down the gradually sloping field. He tossed his mane, he swished his tail, and broke into a canter. The wind and sun caught him in patches of light and shade, he whinnied and turned to gallop up the paddock. Up and down, hooves thudding, he enjoyed the freedom. Sultan made himself at home.

In the far corner, by a stream, stood Solo. He was a small, lonely figure, quietly watching, knowing that it would be all Sultan, Sultan, Sultan with Laura now.

At tea-time the twins said goodbye and promised to come again.

'We've got the rest of the summer holidays to do as we like,' Helen told Laura.

'You can help me with Sultan,' she suggested.

'And Solo,' Hannah added. 'We don't want him to feel left out, do we?'

But as they waved and walked up home with Speckle, throwing a stick for him to fetch, Helen and Hannah both knew that Sultan had replaced Solo in Laura's heart. Solo was yesterday's favourite, the forgotten friend.

'He used to be number one,' Helen said sadly.

'But now he's just second best,' Hannah added.

They could see it clearly, and felt how much it must hurt.

Two

'If that goat goes on making that horrible noise all through the night, I'll have her guts for garters!' David Moore groaned as he strode across the farmyard a few days later.

Sal stuck her head over the wall and snickered.

The twins grinned. 'She's a good alarm clock,' Helen protested. She and Hannah had just fed the hens. Now they pecked and scratched in the yard. The next job was to feed the kittens in the barn.

'An alarm clock only goes off once, when you want it to. That goat goes off all night long!' their father went on.

Sal put back her head and brayed loud and clear. The call echoed up and down the fell.

'See!'

Hannah did a detour across the yard to give the creamy-brown goat a chummy pat. 'She's only being friendly.'

Their dad grumbled on as he headed indoors, camera slung over one shoulder, his old wellington boots scraping on the cobbles. 'With friends like that . . .' he complained.

The twins' mum came out as he went in. She was small and dark like them, with a busy air. 'Never mind him. He had to get up early anyway to take those photographs.'

David Moore took pictures of rare animals and sold them to magazines. He was a wildlife photographer, with a dark-room in the attic. This morning he'd gone high on to the mountain overlooking Doveton Lake to take pictures of a pair of falcons. He'd come back in his shapeless grey sweater, his wavy brown hair wet with dew. He grumbled, but there was a twinkle in his smiley grey eyes. The twins knew that he'd had a successful morning.

'I'm on my way to work.' Their mum stacked boxes

of eggs in the back of the car. 'Hannah, would you remind your dad that the central heating man is coming today?' She gave them each a quick hug. 'And be good, both of you.'

'Aren't we always?' Helen smiled up at her.

'Oh yes, little angels!' Mary laughed. 'And make sure your dad doesn't get into mischief as well.'

They waved as she drove off down the lane. From inside the barn they could hear the four tiny kittens miaowing and scratching at the door.

So the twins went straight in. Helen scooped up a ginger one who tried to escape, and tucked him under her arm. Hannah quickly closed the door. Three other kittens wove in and out between her feet, tails high, miaowing with high-pitched, pleading voices. So far they hadn't had time to find names for them.

'Hold your horses.' Helen put the ginger kitten on to a heap of straw. He wriggled and twisted his way to the floor. Then all four kittens tried to trip her as she bent down for the empty food dish. They had come from High Hartwell, another farm on the fell, from Fred Hunt, the old farmer there.

'What a racket!' Hannah scooped food into the

bowl and put it back on the stone floor. Soon four spiky tails were pointing upwards, four furry heads had disappeared into the large dish and the miaowing had stopped.

'You'd think they hadn't eaten for a week.' Helen rolled up her sleeves and stood back to watch.

'Just think, they'd have ended up at the RSPCA in Nesfield if we hadn't taken them,' Hannah reminded her. Mr Hunt had said he didn't want the bother of finding them good homes. Hannah had gone on about it for days until her mum had given in and said the kittens could come to Home Farm. Now they kept them in the barn until they were big enough to venture out.

The kittens gobbled their food and licked the dish clean. Then they ran their little pink tongues along their front paws and cleaned behind their ears. Lick-groom-lick. Then a roll on the floor, a leapfrog into the straw, and begin all over again. Lick-groom-lick.

'Come on, we'd better go and tell Dad about the central heating man,' Helen said at last.

They stroked the kittens and slipped out through the door. Speckle ran from the house to greet them, to see what the day would hold.

'What shall we do?' Hannah glanced at Lucy and Dandy nibbling at the wet grass by the stream in Sal's field. The geese raised their heads and turned haughtily the other way.

Helen pretended to frown and think. 'Let's see, we could stay in and watch telly?'

'Nah.' Hannah went into the kitchen and poured herself an orange juice.

'We could help Dad develop some films, couldn't we, Dad?'

He sat at the table opening the morning post. 'What? Oh yes, fine by me.'

'Nah,' Hannah giggled.

'Well, we could make ourselves useful around the house, washing up, cleaning, hoovering.'

'Yes!' David Moore's ears suddenly pricked up. 'Hoovering – yes!'

'Nah.' Hannah shook her head.

'I'd pay you,' he offered. Everyone in the Moore family hated hoovering. They would do anything to get out of it.

The twins pretended to consider it. 'How much?' Helen asked.

'Fifty pence.'

'Nah.' They both turned him down flat.

'I know, we could go down and see Laura instead,' Helen said, as if a brilliant idea had struck.

'And Sultan and Solo.'

'Huh.' David opened a big brown envelope and took out a magazine. 'So what's new?'

Every day that week Helen and Hannah had visited Doveton Manor to help Laura get Sultan settled in. They mucked out and cleaned the tack together. Today Laura said she planned to ride Sultan on the fell for the first time.

'Could do, I suppose.' Hannah rocked her head from side to side. 'What do you think, Speckle?'

The dog gave a sharp yap.

'OK then, that settles it,' Hannah beamed. 'Doveton Manor it is.' She began to scout through the vegetable rack by the sink for old carrots to take as a treat for the horses.

'You're sure Laura's parents don't mind?' Their dad flicked through the magazine called *Animal World*, listening absent-mindedly once more. 'Here, take a look at these. Here are some photos that I took. What do you think?' He laid the magazine flat on the table to show them colour pictures of a badger at night.

'Wow!' Helen loved the needle-sharp prints. She could see every hair on the badger's grey coat, every blade of grass underfoot.

'Brilliant, Dad!' Hannah peered over her shoulder.

'Not bad, considering I don't know one end of a badger from another.' He always said he knew nothing about animals, but plenty about cameras.

'Don't you think he looks just like a grumpy old man?' Helen laughed. 'Didn't he like having his picture taken?' She turned the page to see if there were any more. But the next page was full of small adverts and messages from readers.

'That's it, I'm afraid.' David Moore pulled the magazine towards him, but Helen laid her hand flat on the page.

'Wait a minute!' She sounded curious.

'What is it?' Hannah was eager to be off. If they weren't quick, Laura would have already set off with Sultan before they got there.

'I hope that's not Horses For Sale adverts you're looking at,' their dad warned. 'Because if it is, you're wasting your time.'

Helen went quiet as she read the page.

'Why would she be wasting her time?' Hannah wondered what Helen had found that was so interesting.

'Because . . .' He went on to open bills and letters.

'Why, Dad?'

'We can't afford a horse, that's why. As you very well know.' He read one of the bills and blew through his cheeks. 'Not when you see what the central heating's going to cost.'

Hannah remembered her mum's message. 'Oh, by the way—' she began.

'Oh no!' Helen looked up from the magazine, her

face white, her eyes wide. She took a deep breath. 'It can't be!'

'What? What can't it be?' Hannah grabbed the page. 'Where? What are you looking at?'

'That.' Helen stabbed her finger at a small advert in one corner. 'Read it, Hannah!'

Hannah read it out loud. ' "Wanted: Good home for grey pony, 12.2 hands, 11 years, lovely nature." ' It sank in slowly. She looked up at her twin sister. 'So?'

'Read the phone number.'

' "Telephone Doveton 6850." Doveton?'

'Yes, there's a grey pony for sale here in Doveton.'

Hannah felt her stomach churn. 'You don't think . . . ?'

Helen nodded. 'Where's the telephone book?' She ran to the windowsill and brought it back to the table. 'S . . . S?' It slipped open at the right pages. 'San . . . Sar . . . Sau . . . Saunders!' She found the number for Doveton Manor and gasped.

Slowly Hannah read it out. 'Doveton 6850.' She looked up in horror. 'Oh, they can't do that!'

'Can't do what?' At last their dad realised that something was seriously wrong.

'They can't sell him!' Helen and Hannah said.

'Sell who? What's going on?'

It was horrible. They felt as if someone had kicked them in the stomach. 'The Saunders have put an advert in *Animal World*,' Helen explained.

'They want to sell a grey pony. It's Solo. They want to get rid of him!'

Three

'It's not that we want to part with him.' Mrs Saunders looked on as Helen and Hannah fed carrots to Solo over the fence. 'In fact, we'll be very sorry to see him go.'

Not as sorry as Solo will be to leave, Hannah thought. The pony seemed quiet and sad, as if he knew his days at Doveton Manor were numbered. As they expected, Laura had already ridden off for the morning on Sultan, leaving Solo behind.

Helen stroked his soft grey nose. She heard the carrot crunch between his yellow teeth.

'It's the only sensible thing to do in the

25

circumstances.' Laura's mother, a tall, slim woman with blonde hair and a quiet voice, tried to explain. 'Laura has shot up lately and she's grown so tall that Solo was struggling to carry her. Her legs dangled way down below his belly. And of course she can't ride him in shows any more. It was a hard decision, but necessary.'

'And you can't keep him, even now that Sultan's here?' Hannah still didn't see why Solo had to go. All the way down from Home Farm, the twins had been trying to work out why the Saunders had to sell him. After all, they were rich. They lived in a massive house, with a huge garden, a pond, a paddock, stables. Surely they didn't need the money.

'We thought about it long and hard,' Mrs Saunders admitted, 'because we're all so fond of old Solo.'

Not so old, Helen thought. Solo was only eleven – ponies could live to the grand old age of twenty or more.

'But in the end we decided we had to place the advert in the magazine.' Valerie Saunders rested her arms along the top rail of the fence and smiled sadly as Solo came up to nudge her chest. 'Laura's father knows a lot about horses, and he says it would be cruel to keep Solo at the Manor with no one here to ride him. Ponies need to be worked. They should be ridden out every day if possible, otherwise they grow terribly unfit. They get fat and slow. We wouldn't want that to happen to Solo, would we, boy?'

Solo nibbled her top pocket with his rubbery lip.

'And you've had such a nice life so far.' She took another carrot from Hannah and offered it to him. He snaffled it quick as a flash. 'Considering what you were like when we first came across you.'

The twins climbed the fence and perched on either side of Mrs Saunders. They liked her, and knew she wasn't a hard-hearted person as far as animals were concerned. She had a lovely Siamese cat called Lady, and was kind to Speckle whenever they visited. Just now Speckle was roaming among the buttercups, sniffing here and there.

'When Solo came to us,' she told them, 'he was in a sorry state, weren't you, boy? He was six years old when we rescued him from a horse fair. They said he was badly schooled and unreliable.'

'Solo?' the twins cried in disbelief. A gentler, friendlier pony you couldn't hope to meet.

'His first owners found he was too much to handle.

They said he kicked and nipped their little boy, but that was only bad training, of course. And they fed him badly, and the son didn't ride him enough. He was practically a bag of bones, he limped, he had all sorts of things wrong with him.'

'Poor Solo!' Helen stroked his sturdy neck.

'He wasn't called Solo when we first saw him. They called him Quaker. But when we saw him all alone in the middle of the ring, left until last with no home to go to, we decided to call him Solo, and the name stuck.' She smiled at the memory. 'So we bought him and brought him home to Doveton, fed him up and got the vet to call in and keep an eye on him. Soon he was right as rain.'

'And he never kicked or bit after he came here?' Hannah couldn't imagine him ever turning vicious.

'Not once. That's because he got lots of tender, loving care, I expect.'

'We think he's lovely,' Helen murmured.

'But you see why we have to sell him?' Mrs Saunders sighed as she turned to go back into the house.

The twins nodded slowly. 'But what if someone answers the advert, then comes along and wants to buy him, but you know they won't look after him properly?' Hannah ran alongside Mrs Saunders, still worried about Solo's future.

'Oh, we'll make sure he goes to a good home.' She put her hands in her linen jacket pocket and strolled on. 'You don't need to worry about that.'

'And what if no one comes along at all?' Mrs Saunders didn't seem to hear her quiet question, so Hannah fell back to join Helen, Solo and Speckle. 'That's the other thing,' she said, thinking aloud. 'Maybe no one will want to buy him. He'll be homeless all over again.'

'Maybe.' Helen ran a hand through Solo's mane. She began to dream of all sorts of things; of Solo striding along the lakeside, of a space for him in the barn at Home Farm, of herself or Hannah strapping a saddle to his back and riding up on the fell free as a bird, without a care in the world . . .

'Hello, you three.' Laura rode up the drive on Sultan just as the twins and Speckle had decided to go home for lunch. The two of them looked proud and smart – Laura in a tweedy jacket and jodhpurs, Sultan's chestnut coat gleaming in the sun. 'You're not leaving already, are you?'

Hannah mumbled an excuse about having to get back home. They'd left Solo alone in his paddock, kicking his heels and looking bored.

'What's wrong?' Laura swung down from the saddle and took off her hard hat. She shook her hair free and looked from one glum face to the other.

'Nothing.' Helen didn't dare to look her in the eye.

'Yes, there is. I can tell.' She held tight to Sultan's reins to keep him off the neat grass that lined the long drive.

'We read the advert about Solo in *Animal World*,' Hannah said quietly.

'Oh.' Laura sighed and looked downcast. 'That.'

'It's OK, your mum explained.' Helen nodded to her sister that they'd better be going.

'Yes, he needs a younger rider.' Slowly Laura peeled off her riding gloves. 'Poor Solo.'

Everyone felt down in the mouth. Even Speckle lay down and let his chin rest between his front paws, looking dejected. He rolled his big brown eyes from Hannah to Helen and back again.

'Still, I expect we'll find someone nice to look after him.' Laura tried to sound cheerful.

'Won't you miss him?' Helen couldn't resist asking the question.

'Heaps. But I'll have Sultan to keep me busy, won't I, boy?' She reached up to stroke the graceful head, then she turned back to the twins. 'By the way, there was something I've been meaning to ask you.'

They managed to raise their heads and peer out from under their dark fringes. 'Yes?'

'I was wondering, would you like to go on helping me with Sultan and Solo for the rest of the school holidays?'

'What sort of help?' Normally Helen would have jumped in with a loud 'yes!'. But today was different. She didn't know if she wanted to come down to the Manor and find Solo being second best to Sultan, day in, day out.

'It would be more or less what we're already doing – you know, mucking out and grooming. Only I asked Daddy, and he said we should pay for your help, like we'd pay a stable lad. Not much, I'm afraid. But I thought you might want to earn some money, and that way I wouldn't mind asking for your help.'

'You want to pay us for looking after two gorgeous animals?' Hannah let her mouth hang open. 'We'd do it for nothing, you know.'

'Shh!' Helen stamped on her foot.

'What?' Hannah yelped.

'I'll tell you later.' Suddenly her face had taken on a bright, eager look. 'Right, yes, we'd love to. When do we start?'

'Now?' Laura relaxed. She smiled brightly and stooped to pat Speckle.

'Great.' Helen turned in her tracks and headed towards the paddock. 'I'll bring Solo to the stable block. See you there.'

Before Hannah could stop her, Helen climbed the fence and began to coax Solo with a mint sweet covered in fluff which she'd found in the bottom of her pocket.

'I've got a different idea. Wait here.' Laura quickly handed Hannah Sultan's reins and went off. When she came back a couple of minutes later, she carried a saddle over one arm and a bridle slung across her shoulder. 'Have you got him yet?' she called to Helen.

'Here, boy.' Helen softly coaxed Solo. He snickered and sniffed at the sugary mint. Gently she slid an arm round his neck and rubbed his long nose. 'Yes, I've got him.'

'Good.' Laura handed the tack to Hannah and took

Sultan again. 'I'll lead Sultan into the paddock. Will you bring those?'

Hannah nodded and followed. Solo saw them coming and pricked up his ears.

'See, he knows!' Laura laughed, leading the way through the gate. 'Hang on to him, Helen.'

'Knows what?'

'That that's his saddle you're carrying. That's why he suddenly perked up.'

And sure enough, as Laura handed Sultan over to Helen, took the saddle from Hannah and walked quietly up to Solo, he seemed to glow with pleasure.

'About time too.' Laura eased the saddle across his broad back then buckled the girth strap. 'That's what you say, isn't it, Solo?' She worked quickly, explaining to the twins the way things should be done. Soon Solo was saddled up and ready. 'Well,' she said, 'who wants to go first?'

Hannah's mouth hadn't closed properly since Laura had offered to pay them for looking after the horses. Now it hung wide open again. 'You want us to ride him?'

'Someone has to.' Laura tried to hide a smile. 'Since I got Sultan to ride, Solo hasn't had enough work.

You'd be doing me a favour if you learnt to ride him for me. Just until we find a nice new home for him, of course.'

'Me! I'll have a go!' Helen nearly tripped over Speckle in her rush.

'Here, borrow my hard hat.' Laura shoved it on to Helen's head. 'That's right, fasten it up. I'll show you how to mount.'

Soon Helen found herself standing on Solo's left side, facing his tail. 'Are you sure this is right?' She had butterflies in her tummy; Solo's back seemed high and wide from down here, and she seemed to be facing the wrong way.

'Yes, now twist the stirrup strap and put this foot in the stirrup. That's right. Now grab the saddle here and here. OK, I'll give you a leg up. Swing the other leg right across, OK?'

'Ready,' Helen nodded. She seemed to soar high, swung her leg and landed with a thump in the saddle. By some miracle she was now facing Solo's head.

'Fantastic,' Hannah grinned, wishing that she'd bagged first go.

'It's harder than it looks,' Laura warned. 'OK, Helen, now shoulders back, look straight ahead.

Don't try to look down.' She took hold of the pony's bridle. 'Don't worry, he's very gentle, you can trust him. And if you do happen to fall off, you've got my hat to protect your head!'

'Thanks a lot!'

'Right, squeeze with both legs just behind his girth strap. Not too hard, just gently.'

Helen squeezed. To her amazement, Solo began to walk forward.

'Don't hold the reins too tight. Don't look down!' Laura's warnings helped Helen to stay in the saddle. 'Now, squeeze with the left leg and pull the left rein gently. Good. Now, I'm going to let go. You're by yourself.'

Helen swallowed hard. She looked straight ahead and followed instructions. Solo curved gently to the left. Beneath her the saddle creaked and his broad back swayed. In this way they went full circle round the paddock.

'Very good!' Laura came to meet her and showed her how to dismount. All too soon Helen found herself back on firm ground. 'Like it?'

'Loved it!' She took off the hat and blew her hair from her forehead. 'Phew!'

'You looked scared stiff,' Hannah laughed.

'Just you wait.' Helen handed her the hat.

'Your turn, Hannah.' Laura began all over again. 'Of course, you'll need boots and a hat. I expect I can dig some old ones out of the bottom of my wardrobe.'

Hannah sailed through the air on to Solo's back.

'Right, Solo, off you go. Squeeze with both legs, Hannah. A bit harder. That's right.'

The pony moved off, smooth and steady as before.

'Smile!' Helen called. 'I wish I had Dad's camera.'

'Try to look as if you're enjoying it,' Laura smiled.

'I am!' Hannah spoke from the great height of 12.2 hands. She stared straight between Solo's ears and silently prayed.

They spent the whole afternoon in the saddle, then in the stable. Helen learned to trot on Solo, Hannah even had one go at walking the noble Sultan, who was gracious enough to take a beginner on his back, as Laura held his bridle.

Then it was time to lead the horses out of the paddock. The twins' cheeks were flushed with the thrill of it, as they went back to the everyday jobs of mucking out and turning the fresh straw with a pitchfork. Helen filled the haybags and hooked them on to the wall inside the stalls, Hannah gave Solo and Sultan plenty to drink, while Laura took a hoofpick and picked stones out of their feet.

The twins had watched and learned the routine all week. They knew what came next. So Hannah took a dandy brush to Solo and worked from ears to tail, brushing smartly. Then Helen went over this with a body brush, using circular strokes. Laura finished him off with a clean sponge and rounded off with a rub down with a dry cloth.

'See, he loves it!' Hannah smiled and stood back to admire the almost pure white pony. His tail swished, and he snorted happily.

'In here with you,' Laura pushed his nose away from her face and led him to his stall. 'You're just an old softie. Now it's Sultan's turn.' She fastened him in and he poked his head over the half-door. He whinnied softly.

They had to ignore him and get to work on the thoroughbred, starting with his hooves, working hard to get him looking perfect. Sultan too loved all the attention.

'See how vain he is!' Laura caught him trying to get

Hannah to go on combing his mane. 'Don't you know you're already the most beautiful horse in the universe?'

Next door Solo coughed and rattled at his kickboard.

'You just hurt his feelings.' Helen imagined that the clever pony could pick up everything Laura said. He came and stared over the door with big, sad eyes.

Laura's heart softened. The twins watched as she put down the sponge and walked across to Solo's stall. 'I'm sorry, old boy, but what can I do? I can't keep you any more, you know that. I'm too big and you're too little. Like Daddy says, we just have to accept it. It's a fact of life.'

Four

'So, what's going on?' Hannah stretched out on her bed, folded her hands behind her head and gazed up at the ceiling. Speckle was already asleep at the foot of the bed. A silver moon shone through the open window.

'What makes you think there's anything going on?' Helen sounded sleepy. A day's work with the horses had tired her out.

'I just know there is.' Hannah felt she wouldn't have to wait long. Helen could never keep a secret. It was like a fizzy drink; if you shook it, out it popped.

'OK, there is. Do you want to hear it?' Helen sat up

with a grin and hugged her knees. Their beds were close together in the tiny bedroom with its sloped ceiling, and the window that opened on to a giant horse-chestnut tree that rustled in the breeze.

Hannah shifted. She rested on one elbow. 'Is it about Solo?'

'What else?'

'Is it about earning money at the stable?'

Helen nodded. 'It came to me when Laura said she wanted to pay us for mucking out, just like a flash of lightning.'

Slowly Hannah sat up. 'What did?'

'My idea.'

Woken by the sound of their voices, Speckle lifted his head. Outside in the field, Sal brayed into the clear night air.

'So?'

'So, by the end of the holiday we're going to be pretty rich,' Helen explained. 'Lots of lovely dosh.'

'If we work hard,' Hannah agreed.

'But it won't feel like work, it'll feel like fun, being with Solo and Sultan.'

'Especially Solo.'

'So if we earn this money we can save it all up and

buy him.' Helen announced her plan. To her it was
dead simple.

'Hmm.'

'Well?'

'We don't know how much he costs. It didn't tell
you in the magazine.'

'No, but it can't be all that much,' Helen argued.
'Not for one little pony.'

'Maybe not.' Hannah rolled over and stared at her
pillow. Was it too much to hope for? 'We'd better ask
Mum and Dad.'

'Later.' Helen wanted to earn the money before
they told anyone their plan.

'No, now.' Hannah jumped off her bed and went to
lean out of the window.

Speckle joined her. He wagged his tail slowly to and
fro, jumped up and put his speckled paws against the
windowsill. What was Hannah looking at? How could
he know that she was chasing a dream?

'Listen, Helen, if we tell them now that we're saving
up to buy Solo, we'll be able to get them to give us
more jobs.' She wanted to be practical too.

'What sort of jobs?'

'Odd jobs. Washing the car, washing up at the café.'

'Do you think they'd pay us for that?'

'It's worth a try.' Hannah guessed that a pony, even a little one, might cost more than Helen thought. 'We could even do the hoovering!'

'Oh, yuk!'

'Fifty pence,' Hannah reminded her. 'And we could go round the village offering to do jobs for people we know.' There was Luke Martin at the shop, Miss Wesley, their teacher, even bad-tempered old Mr Winter. Then there were the farmers, who always grumbled that they had too much to do. 'Come on Helen, it's worth it. For Solo!'

'I suppose we could advertise: "The Odd-Job Twins. Any job considered. Nothing is too small." ' She warmed to the idea. 'We'd need a name for ourselves.' Absent-mindedly she stroked Speckle's head while they thought.

'I know!' Hannah turned to face her. 'Dogsbody! That's our name. People who do any old jobs – dogsbodies.' Speckle nudged her with his head. 'Yes, you're a clever dog. You gave me the idea for our new name. We'll call ourselves Dogsbody and do the horrible jobs that no one else likes doing. They'll pay us loads of money and we'll save it all up and buy Solo!'

They agreed. They swore they would do it. They would work till they dropped, and nothing would get in their way.

'What on earth's Helen doing with that hoover?' David Moore's jaw dropped when he saw her getting it out of the cupboard.

'She's going to clean the carpet,' Hannah told him with a sweet smile. They'd got up early – there was no time to lose.

'You don't say.' He looked deeply suspicious. 'Mary, come and look at this. Helen's doing the hoovering!' He left his toast and marmalade to follow the twins into the lounge. 'Shall I ring the Guinness Book of Records?'

'Ha-ha, very funny.' Helen flicked a switch and the machine roared.

'It must be a first in the whole of human history! Girl aged ten volunteers to clean house!'

Mary Moore came downstairs with a smile. 'Don't worry dear, I expect they want something.' She slid an arm round his waist, looking fresh and bright in her long white shirt and flowery trousers.

'They do?'

'Yes, I can tell.' The sound of the hoover drowned their voices.

Hannah stood by, all innocence. 'Would you like me to do the dusting?' she asked, as soon as Helen had finished.

Their dad struck his forehead with the palm of his hand. 'Am I really hearing this?'

Mary laughed out loud. 'Next thing we know, you'll be offering to wash my car.'

'Well, actually . . .' Helen began.

Their dad pretended to faint against the doorpost. 'Quick, fetch a doctor!'

'I'll leave you to it,' Mary said. She enjoyed the joke, but it was time to set off for work.

'Oh, before you go . . .' Hannah took a deep breath.

'Ye-es?'

'We were wondering.'

'Uh-oh.' She glanced at David and winked.

Hannah shifted from one foot to the other. She couldn't quite put into words what she wanted to say.

'Fifty pence!' Helen jumped in. 'That's what we charge. It's our rate. Fifty pence for every job we do.'

'Aha!' their mum and dad said together.

'Do you think it's too much?' Hannah said anxiously. 'We could charge less if you think it's too much.'

Helen frowned at her.

'Let's get this straight.' David Moore took them through to the kitchen and sat them down at the table. 'You want us to pay you fifty pence for doing the hoovering?'

'And the dusting and washing the car.' Helen came right out with it while Hannah blushed. 'You said you'd pay us fifty pence!'

'In a rash moment,' he admitted to his wife. 'Yesterday.'

'And what's the money for?' Mary asked. 'There's more to this, isn't there?'

This was where Hannah stepped in. She explained about poor Solo being put up for sale, how it was so sad for him to be pushed out and made homeless again, how they loved the pony and longed to have him at Home Farm.

'Here?' Their mum's face gave nothing away as she sat and listened.

'Yes, there's room for Dad to make him a stable in the barn. And loads of spare grass in Sal's field.'

'And how much will you need to earn so that you can pay for him?'

Hannah and Helen kept their fingers tightly crossed. At least she hadn't said no straight off – no, just forget about it, it's a silly idea.

'We don't know exactly.' Helen kept her chin up. She looked from her mum to her dad. 'But we promise we'll work hard. We'll call ourselves Dogsbody. Anyone can give us work. Fifty pence per job. Can we ask Luke if he wants us to do anything?'

There was a silence. Mary looked at David.

He tutted. 'I don't get this. The twins want to work!'

'Don't tease,' their mum said gently. 'Would you have time? Remember you have to look after all the animals here at Home Farm as well.'

'We'll get up early,' Helen vowed.

'We'll make a plan. We could tick jobs off on a list and write down what we've earned.' Hannah thought ahead.

'What do you think?' Their dad left the last word to their mum.

'You would have to work out how you would pay for the pony's feed and so on. It's not just a question of saving up to buy him. You'd have to look after him for a long time after.'

'We will!' they promised.

'And you would have to be prepared for disappointment. Even if you work very hard, you might not earn enough money to buy Solo.'

They nodded.

'Sure?'

'Yes, as long as you let us try.' Helen didn't really think they would fail. They were very determined.

Another long pause.

'OK.' Their mum nodded. 'OK?' she asked David.

'Yes, you can have a go.'

Hannah and Helen shot to their feet. They hugged their mum and dad. They hugged each other, they hugged Speckle.

'You owe us fifty pence!' Helen crowed. 'For the hoovering.' She opened a cupboard and brought out a round tin. She held it out. 'Put it in the Dogsbody tin!'

The tin was decorated with pictures of ponies, cut out from *Animal World* and stuck on with glue. Round the edges it read DOGSBODY in big red letters. 'The Dogsbody tin?' Mr Moore picked it up and rattled it. It was empty.

'Yes,' Hannah said, sweet as ever. 'It's just something we made earlier!'

Five

Soon after breakfast, the twins descended on Doveton. They were dressed in T-shirts, shorts and trainers, and they headed straight for Luke Martin's shop. Speckle trotted along beside.

'Early birds!' Luke greeted them with surprise as he opened the shutters. Half a dozen white doves perched on the outside of their dovecote and cooed down at them.

Helen and Hannah peered into the dark shop, looking for jobs they could do.

'What are you two up to?' He followed them in.

'Shall we sweep the floor for you?' Helen had

spotted a sweet wrapper in one corner.

'How much?' Luke asked, sharp as a pin.

Here was a man they could do business with. Hannah explained their plan.

'Fifty pence per job?' Luke rubbed his dark beard and hummed. He thought hard. 'There is one thing that needs doing.'

'What?'

'Where?' The twins jumped at it. Speckle sniffed at the doorway.

'Not here. Over at the cricket pitch.' Luke ran the local cricket team and looked after the ground. 'Come this way!' He locked up for five minutes and marched them through the village, down the long main street with its neat slate houses, through the white gate into the pretty cricket ground with its green and white pavilion and smooth green field.

'We've got a match tomorrow,' Luke explained. 'And the day before a match I always roll the pitch.'

Helen looked puzzled. 'Roll on the pitch?' Why would Luke want to do that?

'Not roll on it. Roll it!' He led them to the side of the pavilion where a big iron roller with a long handle stood waiting. 'We use this to flatten the wicket,' he explained.

'Flatten the wicket?' It was Hannah's turn to look confused.

'The wicket. The bit in the middle. It has to be dead flat so the ball bounces true.'

'Bounces true?' The twins shook their heads.

Luke gave up. 'Look, do you want to roll this cricket pitch or not?'

'We do! We definitely do!' They tugged at the big metal roller. It moved half a centimetre.

'Heavy?' He stood grinning.

'No!' They refused to give in. They tugged and pulled until the roller moved another fraction.

'Come round here.' Luke winked and showed them the back of the pavilion. 'Try this.' He pointed to a smaller roller.

To their relief the small one rolled when they pulled it.

'Better?'

'Yep.'

'Right, this is the one we use the day before the match, just to finish things off. Take it out into the middle and roll it up and down a hundred times.

That's a hundred times up and a hundred times down.
Got it?'

They nodded.

'It should take you about an hour.'

They wheeled the roller on to the pitch.

'Come to the shop when you've finished,' he called.
'I'll have the money ready for you.'

So they pulled and pushed, they flattened the short
grass and ironed out every last bump. The sun rose
high and made them sweat. They grunted and
groaned. Fifty-one, fifty-two.

'This is slave labour!' Helen moaned. She wiped her
forehead and eased her aching back.

'Think of Solo,' Hannah reminded her.

'Right. I'm ready.'

They began again, up and down the perfect wicket.
Eighty-nine, ninety. Speckle sat quietly in the shade
wondering what they were up to.

'What shall we do after this?' Hannah asked.

'Die!' Hannah puffed and blew. One hundred!

They put the roller away and staggered back to
Luke's shop.

'You look pretty hot,' he grinned. 'A bit too much
like hard work, eh?'

'No!' they lied.

He opened the till. 'Well done. I didn't think you had it in you.' He handed them a five pound note.

Helen took it and stared at it. 'We don't have any change.'

'And I don't want any. It's yours. You deserve it.' He smiled broadly.

'Five pounds!' They whooped and cheered. Outside, Speckle barked, the doves fluttered and flew off.

'Shall I pass the word round that you want as many jobs as you can get?'

'Please!'

'Dogsbody, eh?'

They nodded. 'No job is too small!'

'You need a business card; name and telephone number.'

'We'll make some.' Hannah was ready to move on. 'See you later, Luke.'

'And thanks.' Helen pocketed the money. Five pounds was a fortune. Soon they would have enough to buy two ponies, never mind one.

That morning they washed two cars and took one dog

for a walk. The dog was Puppy, Mr Winter's Cairn terrier.

'I'm glad to see you doing something useful,' he told them. 'Children these days don't know the value of money. When I was young, I had to work for everything, but now it all comes so easily. TV, videos, these computer games.'

The twins had to listen to him chuntering on. Mr Winter was the retired head teacher at the village school. He still thought that children should be seen and not heard. Now he gave strict instructions on how to take precious Puppy for a walk.

'Keep him on the lead until you get away from the road. Don't let him eat the grass, and don't let him swim in the lake!'

They walked down the street in single file, all prim and proper. Hannah held Puppy on his red lead, Speckle trotted obediently behind Helen. But as soon as they got out of sight on the path to the lake, they relaxed. Hannah let Puppy off the lead. He sniffed and snuffled, scented freedom. His little hairy legs broke into a run. Speckle bounded ahead down to the pebbly shore, straight into the cool, clear water. He yapped with joy.

'Puppy?' Helen looked down at the little dog. He whined and looked up at her. 'What is it?'

'He wants to swim.' Hannah watched Speckle. Only his dark head showed above the water. Underneath the surface, his legs paddled furiously.

Puppy ran to the edge. He dipped his toes in the water. He yelped. Speckle barked and Puppy flung caution to the winds. Barking madly he rushed forward. The shore sloped away; he floated, he swam. His head bobbed, his little legs paddled.

'Uh-oh.' Helen turned to Hannah. 'No swimming, remember?'

'Well, it's hot.' She made an excuse.

'I suppose we could always go in with him and make sure he's safe?' Beneath their shorts and T-shirts, the twins wore their swimming costumes.

So they kicked off their shoes and soon they were all in the lake – twins and two dogs, turning somersaults and splashing in the crystal clear, green water. Then they sat in the sun to dry. It was lunchtime when they took Puppy back home. He was dry, but cleaner than when they set out, the twins thought.

Mr Winter didn't seem to notice. He gave them

their fifty pence and a digestive biscuit as a treat.

'That's what I like to see,' he said. 'Children offering to do things for others. There should be more of it.'

Before he'd finished talking, Puppy had taken to a shady spot in the garden, where he lay down panting hard after his exercise and was soon fast asleep.

'How much?' Helen asked at the end of their first day.

They'd gone on from Mr Winter's to Doveton Manor and spent the afternoon working with the horses. At the end, just before tea, Laura had let them ride Solo again. They both jumped at the chance and felt they were getting better. Mrs Saunders had paid them for their work on the spot: two pounds fifty to add to the rest.

Hannah counted up. 'Nine pounds.'

'Not bad.' She rested against the paddock fence, ready to head for home. Solo and Sultan were still grazing, though soon Sultan would be taken in for the night. There was a pinky-gold glow in the clouds over the fell.

'Red sky at night, shepherd's delight.' Mr Saunders stopped his car in the drive to have a word with the twins. 'Another nice day tomorrow.'

Tired and hungry, but happy, they nodded.

'Laura tells me you're keen on old Solo?'

Another nod. A secret to keep.

'So are we all,' Mr Saunders agreed. 'But you know we have to find him a new home? We're hoping to sell him.'

'How much does he cost?' Helen let the question pop out.

'Quite a lot, I'm afraid.' He smiled, ready to drive on.

'But how much?'

'Four hundred pounds.'

'Four—?'

'Hundred—?'

'Pounds.' Mr Saunders nodded pleasantly. 'But we haven't had any replies to our advert yet, so we'll just have to wait and see.' He drove off smoothly, crunching up the gravel drive towards the house.

Helen and Hannah could have cried. Hannah looked at the five pound note and the handful of coins. They'd worked all day, and they'd earned the grand total of nine pounds.

As if he knew something was wrong, Speckle sidled in between them and gazed up. Solo came across, trotting smartly. Why weren't they going home? He nudged up to the fence and peered over Helen's shoulder.

She put an arm round his neck and hugged him.

Hannah patted him. 'Don't worry, it's not your fault.' There were tears in her eyes.

'And we won't give in,' Helen promised. 'Four hundred pounds sounds like an awful lot of money, but we'll carry on working until we drop to give you a home!'

Six

'You must be really serious about this,' Mary Moore said as she came into the café kitchen with another pile of washing up. Saturday morning was the busiest time at The Curlew. The twins had got up with the lark so that they could drive with their mother into Nesfield to help.

Hannah stood at the sink up to her elbows in soap suds. 'We are.' She pulled a dripping plate out of the bowl and put it on the draining-board.

Helen picked it up and began to dry. 'Dead serious.' Their mum had promised them five pounds for a morning's work. 'Still dirty.' She inspected the plate and slipped it back into the soapy water.

'Hey!'

'It was. It still had jam on.'

'Says you.'

'It did!'

'Didn't!'

'Don't fight, you two.' Their mum stepped in between. 'I think it's time you took a break.' She lifted Hannah's arms out of the water and handed her a towel.

'Ugh, my hands have gone all pink and wrinkly!'

'And I've got blisters on mine from that cricket roller!' Helen showed the evidence – two small sore spots on her palm.

'You're sure you don't want to give in?' Their mum looked worried. 'You don't think you've taken on too much?'

'Course not!'

'You haven't got too attached to that pony, have you?' Her voice held a warning note.

'No-oh!'

She could see that her advice flew in one ear and out the other. 'Well anyway, you deserve a break. Go into town, have a look round. Your dad said he'd call here to collect you at twelve.' She studied them closely. 'Don't worry, you've earned your five pounds.'

The twins gave a sigh of relief. Their total had shot up to fourteen pounds.

'What's four hundred take away fourteen?' Helen asked after they'd left the café and began to head into the town square.

'Three hundred and . . . eighty-six.'

It sounded dreadful. 'Never mind, this is only our second day.' Helen tried to sound cheerful.

They dipped into the edge of the crowds around the market stalls. Local people bustled to buy vegetables, tourists hung around the souvenir shops. But neither Helen nor Hannah cared much about looking.

'I wonder what Solo's doing now?' Hannah drifted down a side street, away from the crowd.

'Eating, I expect.' That's how he spent his mornings, alone in the paddock munching away, while Laura went off on Sultan.

'Well, we'll see him soon.' The plan was for their dad to drop them off at Doveton Manor before he went to play cricket in Luke's team.

'And earn some more money,' Helen said. 'Another two pounds fifty.'

'Every little helps.' Only yesterday this would have seemed like a lot of money. Hannah's attention was taken by a shop they'd never seen before. It had a green sign with the picture of a horse's head, and the words 'Tack and Tuck' written in gold. Instantly the twins were drawn towards it.

'Look at that!' Helen breathed. In pride of place in the window was a brand new saddle, its leather gleaming, its straps and buckles in mint condition.

'And those!' Hannah pointed to a pair of black riding boots, a velvety hard hat and a natty black jacket.

'They don't even have prices on them.' Helen squinted through the window.

They were so busy staring that they didn't see a youngish couple and a boy of their own age coming out of the shop. In fact, as she squeezed into the doorway for a better look at the saddle, Helen bumped right into the red-haired boy.

'Ouch!' He stepped back and rubbed his forehead.

'Sorry.' Helen blushed.

The woman tutted. 'Come along, Mel. Your father's waiting.'

The man stood in the narrow street. 'It's all a bit

pricey,' he grumbled, ignoring the twins.

'Yes, but Mel must have the best equipment. It's very important to have the right outfit, even if it is expensive.' Mum had obviously made up her mind.

The boy glanced at the twins and shrugged. Don't ask me, he seemed to say. I'm only the one who has to wear it.

Helen and Hannah smiled briefly. Funny, he didn't seem the horsey type.

But the family moved on, and after the twins had lingered a few moments longer by the window, admiring the gloves and jodhpurs, they too went back

to the market square to meet their dad.

He was dressed in his 'whites' for the cricket match. 'Wish me luck,' he said after he'd piled them into the car and driven them over Hardstone Pass into Doveton. He drew up outside the big stone gates of the Manor.

'Good luck, Dad.' They jumped out, waiting for Speckle to be let out of the back, but eager to be off.

'Say it as if you meant it.'

'Good luck! We hope you win! We hope you score loads of wickets!'

'Runs,' he corrected. 'In cricket you score runs.'

'Good luck anyway!' They dashed up the drive, climbed the fence into the paddock and ran to meet Solo. They turned once to wave to their dad as the car drove off.

'Solo!' Helen went and threw her arms round his neck. 'You're all by yourself.'

He looked pleased to see them, so they petted him for a while and let Speckle have a run by the stream. Then they decided it was time to get to work.

'Mucking out time,' Hannah sighed.

'Do you want to come?' Helen laughed at Solo. He was trying to follow them through the gate.

'Oh go on, let him.' Hannah couldn't refuse. She held the gate open. Solo trotted ahead into the yard.

'I don't blame you. You're lonely, aren't you?' Helen ran a hand down his neck and gave his shoulder a pat. 'You need someone to talk to.' She led him off to the water trough to drink.

Just then Mrs Saunders came out of the house by a side door. She smiled when she saw the twins. 'Oh good, there you are. And you've brought Solo in from the field.' She looked all around. 'Is Laura still out with Sultan?'

Hannah said they thought she must be. 'We just got here. Solo wanted some company so we brought him in here while we muck out the stables.'

Mrs Saunders glanced at her watch. 'Fine. It looks as if he could do with a good grooming in any case. Can I leave it to you?'

She didn't need to ask twice. Helen and Hannah dived for the brushes and sponges.

'Good. We have to make you nice and smart, don't we, Solo?' Again Laura's mother looked at her watch, then smiled kindly and wandered back into the house. 'Don't forget to knock on the door for your money,' she called from the doorstep. 'I'm

69

expecting visitors. I'll be in all afternoon.'

The twins set to on their favourite job. Solo was going to get a thorough grooming. 'You like it Solo, you old fraud!' Hannah laughed as he refused to lift his foot. 'Come on boy, lift!'

He sighed and did as he was told. Hannah picked at it with a hoofpick. Then they wiped his eyes and face. He wrinkled his nose and snorted. Then out came the brush for his head and neck; long, firm strokes down his chest and forelegs, working along his strong back, under his belly. Last of all came the comb for his long white mane and tail.

'Very pretty!' Helen stood back to admire the final effect.

'Magnificent!' Helen twirled her comb. 'Now you could go anywhere without anyone being ashamed of you!'

Helen turned to the sound of hooves crunching up the drive. 'Hi, Laura! Hi, Sultan! Just come and look at Solo. He's had his beauty treatment.' She wanted to show him off before he got dirty again.

Hannah took hold of Sultan's bridle as Laura dismounted. 'Are you OK?' She thought Laura looked pale and unhappy.

'Yes, I'm fine.'

'You don't look fine.' Hannah led Sultan into the yard. 'Do you want us to groom him for you?'

Laura bit her lip. She seemed to avoid looking at them or Solo. 'Would you mind?'

'Course not.' Helen began unstrapping Sultan's saddle. 'We'll rub him down and get started. He'll soon be good as new.' Laura must have ridden him hard. There was sweat under the saddle, and steam rose from his flanks.

'Thanks.' She ducked her head and dashed into the house.

'She must be feeling ill,' Hannah said. She went for clean sponges to begin on Sultan. 'It's not like Laura to leave him to us.'

They were so hard at work that they took no notice when a big car came up the drive and parked outside the main door. Sultan was playing up, fidgeting as they tried to comb his mane. 'Steady, boy,' Helen whispered in the ear of the highly-strung thoroughbred.

They had just finished and Sultan was looking perfect when the house door opened and footsteps approached. Mrs Saunders and a young couple stood on the patio as Mr Saunders walked over to the stable yard.

'Lovely!' He stroked Sultan's long neck. 'You've done a good job here.' Taking him from Helen, he walked him into the stable. 'Would you take Solo out into the paddock for us?' he asked. 'I'll see you there.'

Puzzled, the twins led the pony across the yard, waiting for the group of grown-ups to join them in the paddock.

'Steady, boy.' Helen spoke quietly to Solo. He seemed restless, unlike himself.

'. . . He's just turned eleven,' Mr Saunders was telling the strangers. 'The twins here have got him into shape so that you can see him at his best. He really is a lovely pony.'

The hairs on the back of Hannah's neck began to prickle. Speckle sat quiet. 'Haven't we seen those people before?' she whispered to Helen.

'I don't know. But I think I know what they want!' She shivered in spite of the warm sun.

'We'd love to keep him here at Doveton Manor, but it isn't practical,' Mr Saunders went on explaining as the group came near. A shorter pair of legs dawdled behind, hidden from view.

'Oh, isn't he gorgeous!' The woman sounded thrilled. Solo stood in the afternoon sunlight, his spotless coat shining. He whinnied nervously and edged up to Hannah.

'I know that voice.' Helen tuned into the high tone. 'Didn't we hear it earlier today?'

'In Nesfield?' Hannah remembered it too.

'Come and look at this gorgeous pony, Mel.' The woman turned to her son. 'See, isn't he lovely?'

The owner of the legs came forward. He looked shyly at the twins. It was the boy with bright red hair.

Mr Saunders opened the gate to let the group in. Looking back at the house, Hannah caught a glimpse of a blonde figure staring down from a bedroom window.

Mrs Saunders left her husband to show Solo off and quietly took the twins to one side. 'That's Mr and Mrs Woodhouse,' she explained. 'They telephoned earlier today to say they were looking for a pony for Mel. They saw our advert in *Animal World*.'

Hannah and Helen wanted to put their hands over their ears and turn away, but Laura's mother went on.

'It seems that Solo could be just the one for them. They seem very interested in him, don't they?'

Seven

'Four hundred pounds, you say?' Mr Woodhouse frowned and looked Solo up and down. 'That seems a bit pricey.'

'But he's nice and gentle.' His wife seemed to have taken to the pony straight away.

'Oh yes, you couldn't get a better natured horse than Solo,' Mr Saunders told them. 'And we do want to make sure he goes to a good home.'

Mrs Woodhouse was keen to impress. 'I'm sure he'd be happy with us. We have a large field at the back of our house, with plenty of shelter. It's ideal.'

'Where did you say you lived?'

'In a little village near Settle.'

The twins hung their heads. Settle was miles away. If the Woodhouses took him there, they would never see Solo again.

Mr Woodhouse was a tall man with short ginger hair. He turned to his son. 'What do you think, Mel?'

'He thinks he's wonderful, don't you?' Mrs Woodhouse never gave the boy a chance to reply.

He nodded silently.

'Come here and stroke him,' she said. 'You'd better get to know him in case we decide to go ahead and buy him.'

Oh, I hope not, Helen prayed.

Say no! Hannah's fingers were tightly crossed behind her back.

Slowly Mel walked up to Solo. He stretched out a nervous hand. Solo tossed his head. Mel stepped back.

His mother made excuses. 'I'm afraid he's not very confident around strange horses yet. But he'll soon get used to Solo. He has riding lessons every week, and they say he's getting much better!'

Hannah looked in dismay at her twin sister. They were right – Mel Woodhouse wasn't a horsey sort at all.

Mrs Saunders stood beside them, watching and listening as the visitors ummed and aahed. She glanced at the house. 'I wish Laura would come down and join us,' she whispered.

'Why won't she?' Helen asked.

'I don't know. I suppose she's too upset about having to say goodbye to Solo. She went out early this morning when she heard that we'd spoken to some buyers on the phone. She didn't even have breakfast.' Mrs Saunders sounded at a loss. 'It must be hard for her. She's had Solo since she was six years old.'

'Maybe they'll decide not to buy him,' Hannah piped up. She could hear Mr Woodhouse arguing over the price. Her hopes rose.

But Laura's mother shook her head. 'Maybe. But someone else will. In the end we have to face it. We need a buyer for Solo, and the sooner the better!'

The Woodhouses stayed for more than an hour. They looked at Solo from every angle, they ummed and aahed some more. In the end they went away saying that they needed longer to think about it. They would decide and get back to the Saunders in a week.

'A week!' Helen wailed. 'We'll never earn four hundred pounds in a week!'

'Three hundred and eighty-three pounds fifty.' Hannah spoke quietly but firmly. The paddock was peaceful. Everyone had gone away and left the twins and Speckle to watch Solo settle down to an evening in the sun.

'We'll never ever do it!' Her stomach twisted into knots. She could hardly bear to look at the beautiful pony.

'So what do we do? Do we just give up?' Hannah cried.

Solo looked up at the sound of her voice. He came slowly towards them to see if there was anything he could do to help. Softly he nuzzled up to Hannah.

Helen began to turn away with tears in her eyes. Then she paused. 'No!'

'No, what?' Hannah rubbed Solo's forehead.

'No, we don't give up!' Helen insisted.

'We can't, can we? Now now.' Hannah spoke softly, but her face looked determined.

'We never gave up over Speckle, did we?' Speckle had been a stray when the twins had rescued him from the quarry and fought to keep him.

'No, and we won't give up over you, Solo.' Hannah didn't know what they could do to earn so much money before the Woodhouses came back, but she set her mind on trying.

'What we need is another big idea,' Helen pointed out. They said their quiet goodbyes to Solo and set off up the lane to Home Farm.

'Dogsbody isn't going to be enough,' Hannah agreed. 'If we had more than a week, the odd jobs would eventually bring in the money. But seven days isn't long, and three hundred and eighty-three pounds fifty is a fortune!'

'A BIG idea!' Helen said again.

'Money, money, money,' added Hannah.

Speckle ran up to them with a sturdy stick and dropped it at their feet. The twins ignored him. He gave a sharp bark.

'Sorry, Speckle.' Helen picked up the stick and threw it in a high arc across one of Fred Hunt's fields. The sheepdog raced to fetch it, ran too far, tripped and bowled over.

Hannah smiled. 'Silly dog.' She called him back. He picked up the stick and came running.

'It wouldn't be so bad if we were grown up,' Helen went on, lost in thought. 'Then we could borrow the money from a bank.'

'Or we'd have a good job and earn lots.'

'Like Dad.' Helen pursed her mouth. 'Photographers earn quite a lot, don't they?'

Hannah's eyebrows shot up and disappeared under her thick fringe. 'If they sell their pictures to a big magazine.'

'Like *Animal World*!' Helen knew that their dad had earned quite a few hundred pounds for his photographs of the badger.

'The pictures have to be special,' Hannah went on.

'You have to have a good camera . . .'

'. . . Like Dad's!'

'Are you thinking what I'm thinking?' Helen's brown eyes began to sparkle.

Hannah nodded. 'If Dad will let us.'

'If we have time.'

'A week.'

'We'd have to be quick.'

'We could do it tomorrow.' The words tumbled out as Helen and Hannah made their new plan.

'Whose picture shall we take?' Hannah wanted to

know. They began to run up the lane. Speckle raced after them.

'It has to be something amazing.' Helen could hardly wait to get it organised. 'An animal that the magazine would love to print a picture of.'

Speckle bounded over the wall to join them in the narrow lane. He flew at it, took it in one magnificent leap, ears back, tail streaming in the wind.

Hannah gasped. Helen clapped her hands. 'Speckle!' they said.

Who better to take a picture of than their own wonderful dog?

All three galloped up the hill and burst into the farmyard. The hens scattered to left and right.

David Moore saw them coming. He opened the door. 'Where's the fire?' he asked.

Helen and Hannah bundled into the house ahead of Speckle. They were breathless with excitement. 'Dad, listen!' Hannah gasped.

'Calm down.' He looked at their flushed faces. 'Take your time. All this rushing around isn't good for me.' He fetched them a cold drink and made them sit down to catch their breath. 'Now, let's see if I can get a sensible word out of you.'

'Oh, Dad, we've just had this brilliant idea!' Helen rushed on like a train. Nothing would stop her now. Their dad would just have to lend them his camera. They would go up on the fell and take Speckle's photograph – somewhere wild, on top of a mountain with miles of rock and sky. It would be a wonderful photograph. The magazine would buy it and pay them hundreds of pounds.

'What do you think?' Hannah waited for Helen to finish telling him their plan. She held her breath. What if he said it was silly even to think about it?

'Well, as a matter of fact' – he rubbed his chin –

'*Animal World* has just written asking me to do more work for them.'

'Oh, Dad!'

'They want a picture for next month's front cover. Something that reminds people of the Lake District.'

'Yes!' They explained their idea about the sheepdog on the mountain. 'With the lake in the distance!' Helen cried.

'It's a rush job,' their dad said. 'I need to get it off before the end of the week.'

'Perfect!' Hannah kept her eyes closed tight. Would he say yes?

'Now.' His voice grew serious. 'We're talking about a lot of money here. This is an important job. If this is going to work out, the photograph of Speckle would have to be all your own work. No help from me.'

'Oh yes!' they agreed. 'That's only fair.'

'And I might have to take my own shots, just in case. I don't want to let the magazine down.'

'Yes, yes!'

'But I would help you to develop and print the film. We'd work together on that.'

'Yes please,' Hannah breathed.

'When can we do it? Tonight?' Helen wanted to know.

'I haven't said yes yet,' he smiled.

'Can we, Dad? Can we?'

'I guess so. If this picture comes out well, I reckon you'll have earned the money fair and square.'

'You hear that, Speckle?' Hannah danced around the kitchen. 'You're going to be a cover-star!'

'When?' Helen's grin nearly split her face in two. 'When can we go?'

'First thing tomorrow, to catch the light.' Their dad folded his arms and enjoyed their excitement. 'An early morning photo-shoot. Set your alarm clock, girls. We have to be up at dawn!'

Eight

'So, who needs an alarm?' Helen poked her tousled head out of the bedclothes. Outside in the field, Sal brayed at the top of her voice. She woke them up before dawn.

Hannah was already out of bed and struggling into her jeans and jumper. 'Hurry up, Helen, we have to be on the fell before the sun rises if we want to get the perfect shot.'

'OK, I'm coming.'

Hannah drew the curtain. A bird whistled sweetly in the dark branches of the horse chestnut tree.

'Are you sure it's not still the middle of the night?'

'No, it's nearly daylight.' Hannah groped under the bed for her trainers. 'I'm off downstairs to brush Speckle's coat and make him look smart. See you down there.'

'Don't go without me,' Helen yawned.

'Well, hurry up, then!'

'Da-dah!' Helen threw back the bedclothes. She was fully dressed, shoes and all. 'Fooled you!' She leapt out of bed.

'Did you go to sleep like that?' Hannah raced her to the top of the stairs.

'What if I did? Are you going to tell on me?'

'Don't argue, you two.' Their mum's sleepy voice drifted out of her bedroom.

'Sorry, Mum!' They charged downstairs.

'No time for breakfast.' David Moore stood barefoot in the kitchen, ready with his camera and a box of spare lenses. Speckle sat by the door, eager for adventure.

'I was going to smarten him up before we set off,' Hannah said.

'Never mind that.' Their dad opened the door. 'He'll just have to look natural instead.'

'You don't think he looks too messy?' She wanted

him to make a good impression for the camera.

'We don't want him to look as if he just stepped out of a dog's beauty parlour, do we?' Helen ran after Speckle into the yard. A tinge of gold appeared on the dark horizon.

Worrying and nattering, bumping into each other, they made their way up the lane.

'Ouch! I can't see a thing.' Helen walked into a tree.

'Look where you're going then.' Hannah decided to follow the white flash of Speckle's tail. He loped ahead until he came to the unfenced, rocky slope of Doveton Fell. Then he stopped to wait.

'I am looking!'

'Follow me. It'll soon be light,' David Moore gasped. He huffed and puffed up the hill in his baggy sweater and wellington boots.

The sun rose in the east from behind the summit of a far-off mountain. Its light crept across the slopes, down into valleys, over the villages. Grey at first, it soon turned a rosy pink.

'Beautiful!' The twins' dad gazed at the sky. 'This is going to be a spectacular sunrise, girls. Are you ready?'

'Should we take it here?' Hannah looked round in

the half-light. They stood on a rocky hillside, near a patch of grass. A few trees caught the sun's first rays. Below them, a long way away, the tiny lake glinted gold.

'Is this wild enough for you?'

'It seems OK.' Hannah felt the butterflies flutter in her stomach as the moment drew near.

'Right. Hannah, you go and sort Speckle out. Helen, you come here and I'll show you how to set the focus.' He twiddled buttons and levers on his expensive camera.

Helen took it all in.

'Most important of all, you must keep a very steady hand. Don't move the camera when you press the shutter. OK?'

She nodded. Her mouth felt dry, but her hands weren't shaking.

Ten metres further up the hill, Hannah got Speckle into position. 'Shall we have him sitting on this rock?'

Helen nodded.

'Here, Speckle. Sit!' She jumped up ahead of him. 'How's that?'

Helen looked at the rock through the camera viewfinder. 'Great. Just let me get a bit higher up, so I

can get the lake in the picture.' She scrambled over loose stones.

'Don't drop the camera!' her dad warned.

'Stay, Speckle.' Hannah jumped to the ground. 'Good boy!' He sat on the rock, ears pricked, interested in everything that went on.

Again Helen pointed the camera. 'Great.' She clicked the shutter. Speckle sat good as gold. 'I've got him in, and that tree behind, and the lake in the distance!' Click, click, click. She flicked the film on from frame to frame.

'How does he look?' Hannah came and hovered at her shoulder.

'Brilliant. Do you want a go?' Reluctantly she handed the camera to Hannah.

'Don't drop it!' Their dad sounded scared stiff.

Then it was Hannah's turn to click away. Speckle sat perfectly still on his rock.

'Dad, watch out!' Helen turned and saw that he was concentrating so hard on his camera that he forgot to look where he was going. He missed his footing, fell flat on his back and began to slide down the slope, feet first. Helen doubled up with laughter.

David Moore slid out of sight with a sudden yell.

Speckle barked. He saw a wavy brown head slide slowly past, and leapt to the rescue. Straight off the rock in one bound, streaking through the air sleek and fast. Hannah clicked. She caught him on-camera, frozen in mid-air; the perfect action shot.

'Ouch, ouch, ouch!'

'Dad!' Helen ran and peered over the ledge. He'd landed on his bottom, right on top of a gorse bush. Helen laughed.

'It hurts! This thing's covered in spikes!' He climbed out of the hollow, grumbling his head off. 'Oh great. I vanish over a cliff, and what do they do? One daughter laughs herself silly, the other cares more about taking the perfect photograph than rescuing her poor old dad! Only the gallant dog tries to help!'

Speckle tried to show him the way out.

'It's not a cliff, Dad. It's a little slope.' Helen tried to set her face straight.

'It may look like a little slope to you, but to me it's a cliff.'

'Are you OK?' Hannah's lip too trembled with laughter.

He looked up at them, brushing yellow flowers out of his jumper. 'Yes, no thanks to you.' He shrugged. 'I suppose it must have looked pretty funny.'

'Whoosh!' Helen giggled. 'I turned round, and there you were, gone!'

'But you got a good shot of Speckle?' he asked Hannah.

She clutched the camera proudly. 'I think so.'

He began to laugh his deep, throaty laugh. 'Well, don't just stand there. Help me up. The sooner I'm out of here, the sooner we can go home and print that masterpiece.'

The sun was up and the sky was blue by the time they'd rescued him and dashed down the fell to Home Farm.

'That's a million times better than anything I could have taken!' David Moore said. They gathered round the dish of printing chemicals watching Speckle's outline appear on the paper.

'Really?' Hannah held her breath. The picture came out crystal clear. She could see every speckle on the dog's front legs as he flew through the air.

'Yes. And the ones of him sitting on the rock. They're pretty good too.'

'No, Hannah's is best.' Helen didn't mind admitting

it. 'Speckle looks brilliant in that one.'

Hannah glowed. 'Is it good enough to send off?'

'Definitely.' He hugged them both. 'Well done.'

'When shall we send it?' Helen watched him take the print out of the dish and clip it up to dry. She wanted an answer from the magazine as soon as possible.

'Let's see. Why don't we drive into Nesfield with your mum. I can take the print into an office. They have a machine for scanning colour photographs. Then they can send it by fax to the editor at *Animal World*. I'll get him to phone me back before the end of the day to tell us whether or not he wants to use it on his next cover.'

'Today?' Hannah's heart leapt into her mouth. 'That's soon.'

'I thought you were longing to know the answer.' David Moore switched off the red safety light and opened the darkroom door. 'Don't you want to know if you've earned the money?'

'We do,' Helen answered slowly. 'But . . .'

'You're nervous. What if he says no?'

They nodded.

He smiled. 'OK, then. How about if I drop you off

in Doveton. You can set about doing your odd jobs for Busybody—'

'Dogsbody!' they said.

'That's it, Dogsbody. Keep busy, like I said, then the time won't drag. I'll do everything in Nesfield, get the fax sent off. Then I'll come and pick you up about lunch-time. How's that?'

They agreed, and went down to grab breakfast while the photographs dried.

'What do you really think?' Mary asked, practical as ever. 'Does the picture stand a chance?'

He took a deep breath. 'It's a very good picture. But we'll just have to wait and see.'

'And don't get your hopes up too high,' their mum warned. 'Remember, it won't be the end of the world if these other people, the Woodhouses, end up buying Solo instead.'

'Yes, it will!' Helen mouthed at Hannah and vice-versa.

'Let's keep our fingers crossed.' Their dad went upstairs to fetch the photos.

They promised to be patient. But having to wait a whole day to find out was going to be agony.

'Come on, into the car everyone. Let's go.' Mary

held the doors open. Their dad came downstairs with the precious envelope and the twins climbed into the car with Speckle.

'Did anyone say well done to you, boy?' Mary asked as he leapt obediently into the back.

They turned to fuss him. 'Oh yes, Speckle, you were great!'

'We couldn't have done it without you!'

'You're a star.' Hannah hugged him.

'A pin-up,' Helen giggled.

Speckle wagged his tail like mad.

'We hope!' their mum said. She started the car and drove out of the farmyard. 'But, remember, let's not count our chickens before they've hatched!'

Nine

'Laura's out,' Mr Saunders called to the twins from the lawn in front of Doveton Manor. He trimmed the edges while Mark, the gardener, used the big mower.

'With Sultan?' Helen asked. They were heading for the stable to fetch Solo's tack.

'How did you guess?'

She grinned. 'Is it OK if we ride Solo in the paddock?'

'Fine. Go ahead.' He came into the yard with them to help with the saddle.

'Have you heard from the Woodhouses yet?' Hannah asked quietly. Mr Saunders scared her. He

97

was tall and straight like a soldier, a bit strict.

'Not yet. Why?'

Hannah blushed. She longed to jump in with their offer to buy Solo, but she couldn't – not yet.

'I suppose you'll be sorry to see him go too,' he admitted. 'We can hardly get a word out of Laura these days because of all this.' He waved a hand at Solo then glanced up at the sky. There were dark clouds over the fell, the first for many days. 'It's going to rain. She'll get soaked through if she's not back soon.' He slung the saddle over the fence. 'Better get on,' he said, and left them to it.

'Cheer up, Solo,' Helen called to him from the far side of the field. He plodded heavily towards them.

'Poor old thing.' Hannah reached out to stroke his neck. 'You're lonely, aren't you?'

Soon though, with Speckle running about in the field and the twins saddling him up for work, the pony grew more cheerful.

'You need company, that's what you need.' Helen talked as she worked. 'And with a bit of luck that's what you'll have from now on.'

'I wonder how Dad's getting on?' Hannah checked the girth strap while Helen put on the hard hat.

'We'll soon know.' She swung into the saddle, determined not to show how worried she felt.

And for the rest of the morning, until their dad came to pick them up, they worked Solo hard, walking then trotting him around the paddock, first Helen, then Hannah taking it in turns to give him plenty of exercise.

By lunch-time the clouds that Mr Saunders had spotted above the mountain had gathered. They rolled down the fell into the valley. It grew misty and damp, a real Lake District day of drizzle and fog.

'Isn't Laura back yet?' asked Mrs Saunders in the yard as the twins got ready to go home. Their dad had called to collect them, saying that he had sent the photo off from the office in Nesfield. Now all they had to do was to sit at home and wait for the phone to ring.

'No.' Helen looked up at the sky.

'Oh dear,' Laura's mother sighed. 'Normally I wouldn't worry. She's an excellent horsewoman. She was practically born on a horse's back. But Sultan isn't used to being out in this weather. He likes sunny days. I'm not sure how he'll behave in the mist.'

'We'll try and spot them as we go up to Home

Farm,' Hannah offered. 'If we see her, shall we tell her to come straight home?'

'Yes please.' Mrs Saunders looked grateful. 'She doesn't usually stay out this long. I hope nothing's happened to her.'

'I'm sure she'll be all right.' David Moore looked on the bright side. 'Like you say, she's a good rider, and she knows her way about the fell.'

Mrs Saunders nodded. 'I'm probably worrying about nothing.'

Hannah hovered by the car. She couldn't wait to get home. She wanted to be there in case the man from *Animal World* rang.

So they got Speckle into the back of the car and drove up the lane through the drizzle towards Home Farm.

'No sign of Laura and Sultan.' Helen peered through the swish and whir of the windscreen wipers.

'I can hardly see a thing,' Hannah said. 'I wish this rain would stop. They must be getting soaked.'

'She'll probably be home by now,' their dad said. 'If she had any sense, she'd come down off the fell as soon as the clouds rolled in.'

'Hey, is that the phone?' Helen leapt from the car as soon as it pulled up in the farmyard. 'No, sorry. False alarm.' She blew her damp fringe from her face and went to let Speckle out.

'I'll put the kettle on.' David opened the door and kicked off his muddy shoes. Hannah slipped away to check the kittens in the barn.

Minutes ticked by. Half an hour. An hour.

'What if he says no?' Helen whispered. She watched the hands of the kitchen clock edge forward. Some-where in an office in the middle of London, a man who knew nothing about their problem was deciding Solo's fate.

'You mean, what if he doesn't want the photo?' David asked.

'Don't!' Hannah couldn't bear to hear him say it.

'Dad, phone!' Helen shot out of her skin. It echoed through the whole house.

'I'll get it.' He picked it up. 'Yes, speaking . . . yes, I've got that . . . our own dog, as a matter of fact . . . Speckle . . . this morning. Yes, OK. Well, thank you very much.' He put down the phone with a click.

The twins held their breath, they stared hard at their dad's face, trying to read the answer.

'He wants to buy it!'

Silence for a split second. Then the twins jumped in the air like footballers who had scored a goal. They leapt and punched the air. 'Yes!'

'How much?' Helen danced with Speckle.

'Two hundred and fifty.' He repeated the offer.

'Two hundred—'

'—And fifty!' It was a fortune.

'Is it enough?' he asked.

'No.' Helen came to earth with a bump.

'We've already earned nineteen pounds.' Quickly Hannah did the sum in her head. 'That makes two hundred and sixty nine pounds altogether. But they want four hundred pounds for Solo.'

'Perhaps you can bargain with Geoffrey Saunders,' their dad suggested. 'See if you can get him to bring the price down.'

'Now?' Helen already had the phone in her hand.

'Why not?'

Hannah stood with both hands over her mouth. 'Oh please say yes!' She closed her eyes and waited.

'Hello, Mrs Saunders? This is Helen Moore.' The words gushed out. Helen hopped from foot to foot. But something stopped her in her tracks. She listened hard. 'Yes . . . no, we haven't.' The smile fell from her face.

'Make the offer!' Hannah breathed. What was happening? What had gone wrong now?

'Sultan? . . . Yes. No, OK, I'll tell Dad . . . Yes, thanks, bye.' Her voice was flat as she put down the phone.

'What?' Hannah's heart had sunk. Something dreadful had happened, she knew.

Helen swallowed hard. 'It's Laura. She still hasn't come back home.'

'Maybe she decided to stay under shelter until the

rain stops?' their dad suggested. But even he sounded worried.

She shook her head. 'No. They think there's been an accident. They've got lots of people out looking for her.'

'What kind of accident? How do they know?' Hannah knelt beside Speckle and put her arm around him.

'Sultan came back half an hour ago, without his rider.' Helen's eyes were wide and scared. 'His saddle had slipped and his knees were grazed. They think Laura must have fallen. She's lost on the fell!'

Ten

'Speckle, here boy.' Hannah recovered from the shock of hearing the bad news and got to work. She raced out to the car and grabbed Laura's old riding hat which she'd bundled into the boot along with their wellingtons and jackets. She showed Speckle the hat and let him sniff it.

'Find her, Speckle. Find Laura.' Helen knew what Hannah was up to. 'Dad, come on, we have to go and look for her.'

'I'll just scribble a note for your mum.' He zipped his jacket and locked the door. 'One good thing, I think the rain's easing off.'

'Did Mrs Saunders say where the others had started looking?' Hannah was satisfied that clever Speckle understood what he had to do. He finished sniffing at the hat and ran into the lane. He barked, ran back to them, urged them to follow him.

'Yes, along the bridle path up to the top of the fell. There're about ten people in the search party.'

'Have they called in Mountain Rescue?' David wanted to know how serious the situation was.

Helen nodded.

'Go on then, Speckle, show us the way!'

They set off at a run through the drizzle and mist.

Helen took the lead, close on Speckle's heels, up on to the open hillside. He sniffed and searched out Laura's scent, nose down, zig-zagging across the hill.

'Thank heavens, the sky's getting lighter.' Hannah knew it would make the search easier.

They splashed through steams and climbed slopes of loose, slippy stones. Speckle's trail took them high on the fell from rock to rock, between trees and bushes, higher and still higher.

'You're sure he knows what he's doing?' David Moore had to pause to catch his breath.

The twins nodded. 'Yes, but he hasn't picked up the scent yet.'

Hannah pushed her hood back from her head. 'The rain's stopped.'

Mist swirled into the valley, but up on the fell the sky had cleared.

'Come on!' Helen watched Speckle keep his nose to the ground. Suddenly he began to sniff hard in one small area, close to a large black boulder. 'I think he's found something!'

They ran as fast as they could. Speckle crouched and waited. Helen got there first and stooped to pick up a light coloured glove, wet through after the rain.

'It's Laura's!' Hannah recognised it straight away. 'Good boy, Speckle!' She waited for their dad to join them.

'But this is way off the bridle track.' He took the glove and turned it over. 'Perhaps we should try and find the Mountain Rescue team and tell them they're on the wrong track?'

The twins disagreed. 'No time.'

'Laura could be lying injured somewhere.'

'Listen.' Helen made up her mind. 'Dad, you go for the rescue team, bring them across. We'll stay here and keep on looking.'

'Yes.' Hannah looked round. 'I think I know where we are now. Look, there's the quarry where we first found Speckle.' She pointed to a rocky scree a few hundred metres to the left.

'Laura's round here somewhere.' Helen watched Speckle continue the search, twisting this way and that to pick up the scent.

'OK.' David agreed at last. 'Don't move away from this area. I'll be as quick as I can.' It would take him half an hour to reach the bridle track on the far side of the fell.

'Hurry up, Dad.' Helen had already set off after Speckle.

'And you two be careful, you hear?'

Hannah nodded and followed the others. Soon they'd crossed the scree. David meanwhile took the opposite direction and disappeared down the slope.

Speckle searched eagerly until he came to a steep ledge near the top of the hill. The ground dipped away suddenly. He stopped, turned and whimpered.

The twins joined him, breathless and scared. 'What is it, boy?'

He yapped once, trotted along the ledge, came

back, barked down into the deep quarry.

'Oh no!' Helen stared at Hannah.

'She must be in there!' They gazed down the rough, jagged sides into a jumble of bushes, wrecked cars, weeds and rusting farm machinery in the bottom.

'She must have fallen.' Hannah held on to Speckle's collar. 'Shh. Good boy.'

'Or else Sultan threw her off.' In the mist, in the rain, sensing a sudden drop under his feet, he could have reared and thrown her off. Then the riderless horse had headed home alone.

'Laura!' Hannah shouted then listened. She caught her own echo. 'Laura-aura-aura!' Nothing.

'Laura-aura-aura-aura!' Helen had a go. Speckle barked and dipped down into the steep sided quarry.

'Here!' a faint voice answered this time. 'I'm down here.'

'Laura?' Helen scrambled after Speckle.

'Here.' She sounded a long way off.

The twins followed Speckle down the slope. Stones slid and slipped underfoot. Sometimes they half-fell, grabbed onto wet bushes to stop themselves from hurtling down. 'Laura, we're coming. Where are you?'

They followed her voice. Speckle leapt the final few metres on to level ground.

'Over here! By the car. I'm trapped.'

They found her at last, half under an old car, wedged against a rusting wheel. She was caught by a piece of sharp metal. It had ripped through her trousers, and now a slow trickle of blood dripped down her knee.

'Are you sure you can't move?' Helen crouched down and looked under the rusting shell.

'No.' She shook her head. 'I must have been knocked unconscious. Sultan bolted, up by a big rock. I lost my riding-crop, my glove. Then he reared up, I fell off, slid down a slope and then I don't remember a thing until I woke up with my leg trapped in here.'

'Don't worry, we'll soon get you out.' Helen knew that Laura must be trying to hide how much her leg hurt.

'How did you find me?' she gasped. Her face was white with pain.

'Speckle did it. He tracked you down.'

Laura managed a faint smile. Speckle went over for a pat. He nuzzled against her cold, wet cheek.

'Dad's gone off to fetch the rescue party.' Hannah took hold of her hand. 'They'll soon be here.' She told

Helen not to try to move Laura's leg in case it was broken. 'We'd better wait for a doctor. Are you sure you can hang on?'

She nodded. 'I'm all right now that you're here.'

'Your mum was worried sick,' Helen said.

'How's Sultan?' She held hard on to Hannah's arm.

'He's fine. A few scratches on his knees, that's all. Everyone's out looking for you.' Hannah managed to catch Helen's eye. 'Shall we tell her?' she whispered.

'Tell me what?' For the first time since they'd discovered her, Laura's mind was taken off the pain of her injured leg.

'You tell her,' Helen whispered. She crouched beside Speckle, who sat with his tongue lolling. 'You're the one who took the photo.'

'What photo?' Laura tugged Hannah's sleeve.

At the top of the slope, growing nearer, they could hear men's voices, feet tramping across loose stones. 'Laura! Hannah! Helen!' they yelled.

'What photo? Please tell me!' Laura ignored the voices.

Hannah nearly burst with pride. 'We've earned loads of money from a picture we took of Speckle. We want to buy Solo from you, then he can come and live with us at Home Farm!'

Eleven

That evening, Helen and Hannah and their parents stood in the stable yard at Doveton Manor.

The Mountain Rescuers had scrambled into the quarry, freed Laura from the wrecked car and carried her to safety. At hospital in Nesfield she had six stitches in the wound in her leg. Nothing was broken. She was lucky, they said.

'Never stay out on the mountain in bad weather,' the team leader told her. 'It's asking for trouble.'

Laura said she was sorry, she'd been feeling upset, and lost track of where she was when the rain began. But now she was safe at home. She sat on the terrace in the quiet evening light, gazing at Solo and Sultan in the paddock.

'I won't do it again,' she promised her parents. 'It wasn't Sultan's fault though. It was mine. I kept him out too long, then we got lost in the mist. He stumbled, missed his footing and bolted. You won't blame him, will you?'

Mrs Saunders sat down beside her. 'No, we're just glad you're safe.'

'Thanks to Speckle,' Laura told them the whole story of the rescue – how the twins' clever dog had picked up her trail and followed it to the quarry.

Hannah beamed at Helen. 'Our dog did it,' she whispered proudly.

'He rescued our friend.'

'And he's about to be a star.'

He sat between them, head up, ears pricked.

'How can we ever thank you?' Mrs Saunders smiled up at the twins, then at their mum and dad. 'Your girls have been marvellous. We'd like to repay you.'

Mr Saunders, still dressed in his waterproof jacket and boots, agreed. 'Anything. You can have anything you want as a reward.'

'Well?' Mary nudged Helen. 'Now might be the time to make your offer.'

For once Helen was tongue-tied. She looked to Hannah for help.

'Laura knows what it would be,' Hannah said. 'We've already told her.'

All faces turned to the patient.

'Well?' Mrs Saunders waited patiently.

'Helen and Hannah have put in an offer for Solo,' Laura announced. 'They want to buy him for two hundred and sixty-nine pounds.'

Hannah felt dizzy. Helen's mouth was dry. They were one hundred and thirty-one pounds short of the price Mr Saunders wanted for the pony. Did they have any chance? Two pairs of anxious brown eyes stared in his direction.

'You don't say!' Laura's dad stepped back and clasped his hands behind his back. 'Of course, you know the asking price is four hundred pounds . . .'

'We realise you might want time to consider it,' Mary said calmly. 'We don't expect an answer straight away. Especially since there's another family interested in buying him.'

No! The twins scarcely dared to breathe. Now was

not the time to be polite and reasonable.

But Mrs Saunders stood up and took her husband to one side. He listened and nodded. She turned to face them. 'No, we don't need time to think about it.'

Helen's heart dropped into her boots. Hannah couldn't look up. They stood in absolute misery.

'We'd be delighted to let Solo come to you. We'd love the twins to have him at Home Farm.'

'You're sure?' David's face creased into a smile.

'Positive.' The grown-ups shook hands.

The twins stood there stunned.

'In fact,' Mr Saunders began, (as if his was the final word) 'we won't accept a penny for him. You two must have the pony as a present, a reward for helping us today.'

Helen gasped. Hannah swung round to look at Laura, who nodded happily.

'We want you to keep your hard-earned money,' he said kindly. 'Ponies cost plenty to keep, you know. You'll have to buy him feed in the winter. It's not cheap.'

'And what about the Woodhouses?' Mary reminded them.

Mr Saunders shrugged. 'They missed their chance, I'm afraid. And to tell you the truth, we didn't really take to them. No, I'm sure Solo will be much happier at Home Farm.'

Slowly the truth sank in. First Hannah, then Helen, then Speckle broke away from the group on the terrace. They ran towards the paddock. Behind them voices drifted in the still air.

'I'll bring Solo up to the farm first thing tomorrow morning,' Mr Saunders promised.

'I can't think of anywhere better for him to live,' Laura said. 'With you and all your other animals.'

'Yes,' David Moore laughed. 'We've got quite a crowd.'

'. . . Lucy and Dandy,' Helen explained to Solo, who trotted across to meet them. 'They're the geese. And Sugar and Spice the rabbits.'

'. . . And the kittens. You can help us choose names for them. And Sal the goat. You'll share her field. Watch it, because Sal can be a bit of a bossy boots sometimes.' Hannah could have sworn that Solo understood every word.

Speckle wagged his tail and jumped through the fence posts. Solo whinnied and nodded his head.

'. . . Oh, and Speckle!' the twins chimed together. They looked at each other and spoke as one, 'Our hero. How could we possibly forget about you!'

Another Hodder Children's book

If you've enjoyed this book, look out for the other books in the Home Farm Twins series.

SPECKLE THE STRAY

Jenny Oldfield

A lost puppy, trapped in a dangerous quarry! Has he been abandoned there?

The twins long to keep him – but what if the owner comes back?

If you've enjoyed this book, look out for the other books in the Home Farm Twins series.

SINBAD THE RUNAWAY

Jenny Oldfield

Sinbad needs a home while his owner is on holiday.

The twins adore the fluffy black cat, but he leaves a train of chaos wherever he goes!

And then he runs away.

Can Helen and Hannah find him – before he gets into real trouble?

Home Farm Twins
JENNY OLDFIELD

❏	661275	Speckle The Stray	£3.50
❏	661283	Sinbad The Runaway	£3.50
❏	661291	Solo The Homeless	£3.50
❏	661305	Susie The Orphan	£3.50

All Hodder Children's books are available at your local bookshop or newsagent, or can be ordered direct from the publisher. Just tick the titles you want and fill in the form below. Prices and availability subject to change without notice.

Hodder Children's Books, Cash Sales Department, Bookpoint, 39 Milton Park, Abingdon, OXON, OX14 4TD, UK. If you have a credit card our call centre team would be delighted to take your order by telephone. Our direct line is *01235 400414* (lines open 9.00 am – 6.00 pm Monday to Saturday, 24 hour message answering service). Or you can send a fax on *01235 400454*.

Alternatively please enclose a cheque or postal order made payable to Bookpoint Ltd to the value of the cover price and allow the following for postage and packing:
UK & BFPO – £1.00 for the first book, 50p for the second book, and 30p for each additional book ordered up to a maximum charge of £3.00.
OVERSEAS & EIRE – £2.00 for the first book, £1.00 for the second book, and 50p for each additional book.

Name ....

Address ....

....

....

If you would prefer to pay by credit card, please complete:
Please debit my Visa/Access/Diner's Card/American Express (delete as applicable) card no:

Signature ....

ExpiryDate ....